I Was There...

ROYAL NURSEMAID

...ted and bound by CM Group (UK) Ltd, Croydon, CR0 4Y...

1 3 5 7 9 10 8 6 4 2

...Phil Adams to be identified as the author of this work has bee...
...in accordance with the Copyright, Design and Patents Ac...

This book is sold subject to the condition that it shall not, by way of...
...the first sends, resold out, or otherwise circulated without the...
...or in any form or binding other than that in which it is publi...
...similar condition, including this condition, being imposed o...
...subsequent purchaser.

While this book is based on real characters and actual historical events, some
situations and people are fictional, created by the author.

Scholastic Children's Books
Euston House,
24 Eversholt Street
London, NW1 1DB, UK

A division of Scholastic Ltd
London ~ New York ~ Toronto ~ Sydney ~ Auckland
Mexico City ~ New Delhi ~ Hong Kong

First published in the UK by Scholastic Ltd, 2014

Text copyright © Jill Atkins, 2014

Illustrations by Michael Garton
© Scholastic Ltd, 2014

ISBN 978 1407 14505 1

Pri   Y

The right o   en asserted
by her   1988.

This boc   rade or
otherwise k   publisher's
prior cons   ished and
without ;   pon the

I Was There...

ROYAL NURSEMAID

Jill Atkins

SCHOLASTIC

PROLOGUE

My mother says I'm a very lucky girl and I think she's right. There are so many girls who would love to have my job. Not many girls can say they have been where I have been and seen what I have seen.

My name is Charlotte, but I like to be called Lottie, and I work in the best place in the world, Buckingham Palace. Even better than that, I'm nursemaid to Princess Victoria, the little daughter of Queen Victoria and her husband, Prince Albert. I began my job several months ago when the princess was only a few months old.

Of course, I'm not the only one looking after Princess Vicky. Mrs Roberts is Head Nurse. She is quite plump and motherly and really friendly. She has been very kind to me since I started here.

I'm really glad that Jane, the other nursemaid, and I do everything together, carrying out our chores and caring for the little princess. Jane is so full of fun and enjoys teasing me and making me smile. We've become the best of friends.

CHAPTER ONE

I love living and working at Buckingham Palace. I'll never forget that morning, after I'd been there for a few weeks, when we heard some really exciting news.

"Lottie, Lottie!" Jane rushed up to me as I was opening the windows in the nursery, as I did every day. Mrs Roberts had taken little Princess Vicky out for her morning walk and it was my job to air the rooms while they were gone. Jane leant forward to whisper in my ear. "I've just heard something really amazing."

She sounded so excited it made my fingers tingle. "What?" I whispered.

"Well, I was talking to one of the chamber maids and she told me…" She stopped there and grinned.

"What did she tell you?" I put my hands on my hips and rolled my eyes. I had already learned that Jane loved to gossip, and she also enjoyed teasing and keeping people in suspense.

"…Queen Victoria is expecting another baby!"

"Gosh!" I said. "That *is* wonderful news!" I smiled. "Having two little royal babies to help look after is going to be even more perfect than one."

That afternoon, Queen Victoria came up to the nursery to see Vicky. Her Majesty is a very small lady with dark brown hair parted in the middle, and pale blue eyes. She was wearing a cream silk dress with folds of lace around her shoulders and arms. I am not sure whether I dare say it, but I had noticed she was getting a little plump. It must have been the baby growing inside her.

The news that the queen was pregnant spread fast amongst the servants and maids, but none of us knew when the baby was due to be born. But a few days later, Mrs Roberts called Jane and me to the nursery while Vicky was asleep.

"I expect you have both heard the happy news?" she began quietly.

I gripped my hands together, hoping she would not be cross with us for gossiping, but Jane didn't look worried. She smiled at Mrs Roberts.

"We heard the queen is going to have another baby," she said. "Is that right?"

"Yes, Jane. The doctors say it is due in November, just before the little princess's first birthday."

"That's only three months away!" I said. I couldn't wait for the new prince or princess to be born.

CHAPTER TWO

Three months passed very quickly and November arrived with its colder days, thick London fogs and darker evenings. The lamplighters came early each afternoon, climbing their ladders and lighting the flickering gas lamps along the streets, and the leaves on the trees turned brown and gold.

I grew more and more excited as we all waited impatiently for the new baby.

By November, I had made other friends, too, Mary and Eliza. Mary was one of the queen's maids who had a shock of wild red hair that kept escaping from underneath her cap, while Eliza worked as a housemaid. She giggled a lot and kept reminding me I was the youngest person working in the palace.

"I'll keep you under my wing," she said.

That made me chuckle. She was not much older than me and she couldn't read or write so she had to ask me to read things to her. I even wrote letters to her mother for her. It was more like *me* looking after *her*!

Then one day, when I went down to the kitchens, I met a girl I didn't recognize. Her thin face was very pale and she was biting her fingernails and staring around her like a lost sheep.

"Hello," I said.

She didn't answer and I could see she was trying not to cry.

"Are you all right?"

She nodded then shook her head.

"I'm Lottie," I said. "I'm nursemaid to Princess Victoria."

The girl sniffed. "Susan," she muttered. "I'm the new scullery maid. But... but I've

never been away from home before and…"
She burst into tears. I put my arm around
her shoulder.

"You'll soon get used to it," I said.
"I'll never forget my first day here. I was
terrified."

It was true. I remembered it very well. On
that first day, Jane had said almost exactly
the same to me. My hands were shaking
like leaves in the wind and my mouth was
so dry that my voice had a strange squeak
when I said, "Hello". Jane must have noticed
how nervous I was.

We had climbed upstairs to Princess
Vicky's nursery, on the top floor of the
palace, right next to the room Jane and I
were going to share.

"We all have to be ready to leap out of
bed and run to Princess Vicky if she wakes

up during the night," she said as she opened the door to the nursery.

I stood in the doorway looking in. It was a rather dismal room with a small window on the right. There was a big oblong fireguard around the fireplace, a table and three chairs on one side of the room and a chest of drawers and a small wardrobe on the other. The princess's cot was opposite the door. It had a wooden frame and basket-weave sides.

"We spend most of our time in here with the princess," said Jane.

"I'm really looking forward to meeting her," I said, feeling that tingling in my fingers that I always get when I'm really excited.

"Come on," said Jane. "I'll help you get dressed in your uniform."

We went to our room. There was just enough space for our two narrow beds, a dressing table and a wardrobe.

Jane waited patiently while I changed into my uniform. I had to wear a cotton petticoat under my dark ankle-length cotton dress, and a waterproof apron under my white one. My hands were trembling, but I felt very proud of myself when I had tucked my curly brown hair under the little white cap and I stood looking at myself in the wardrobe mirror.

"You look the part," Jane said. "Ready to start work?"

I smiled at her. "Will you tell me what

I have to do?"

"Of course. First, I'll show you where everything is." She opened a cupboard on the landing outside our room. Inside, we found carpet beaters and feather dusters, brooms and brushes, buckets and mops, the coal bucket and fire tongs. She told me about the chores I would have to do every morning.

"How many people look after Princess Vicky?" I asked.

"Well, apart from us, there's Mrs Roberts, who's Head Nurse... and Mrs Southey, who's Superintendent of the nursery and in charge of all of us. She's rather strict, but she is not here very often." Jane grinned. "She's really old and wears eyeglasses. You might have met her at your interview."

I nodded. "Oh yes, I remember her... who else?"

"Doctor Clark. We call him if the princess

is not well. And last, there's Baroness Lehzen."

"Who is Baroness Lehzen?"

"She used to be Queen Victoria's governess when she was a little girl. The baroness just keeps an eye on us. She has her own room here in Buckingham Palace, next to the queen's." She looked over her shoulder to check that we were alone. "She has rather a pointy nose and chin. And… I've heard Prince Albert doesn't like her at all."

My brain was buzzing. There was so much to remember.

"I'll show you around," said Jane. "Normally, we'd go down the back stairs, but as it's your first day, we'll take the grand staircase."

It must be the most beautiful staircase in the world. When I first saw it, it took my breath away. I stood at the top and stared at the two flights of stairs, one curving down on either side of me. My fingers tingled as I touched the dark handrail and noticed the intricate pattern of carved golden leaves underneath it. Then, keeping my chin up and my back very straight, I felt like a queen as I walked down the right hand stairs.

"Now, Queen Lottie," Jane whispered, "I'll show you around the parts of the palace where we're actually allowed to go."

On our way to the kitchens, the laundry room, the servants' dining room and several other places, I stared open-mouthed at the wonderful rich carpets, the ornate furniture and the portraits that hung on the walls.

"Try not to get lost," she warned. "And never ever stray into the queen's private chambers."

"What would happen if I did?" I asked.

"They'd send you to the Tower of London and chop off your head!"

I stared at her. She looked so serious that I couldn't help but believe her.

Then she giggled. "I'm only joking. Goodness, if you could see your face!"

After that, we went to the laundry room where some of Vicky's clothes were waiting to be ironed. I heated a heavy flat iron in front of the fire. The clothes, especially the frills, were so tiny and delicate I had to be careful not to scorch them, but when I had finished, I was pleased with my first effort and Jane said I had done a grand job.

"Tomorrow, we start early," she said with a grin.

Suddenly, Susan coughed and I snapped out of my daydream and looked at her again. She had stopped crying and her face was not so pale now.

"I love it here," I said. "My life is so busy. I don't feel at all homesick."

"What's it like, looking after the princess?"

"Wonderful!" I said. "I wouldn't change my job for all the world."

"It must have been marvellous, meeting a real live princess."

"It was," I said. "But I had to wait. I didn't meet her until my second day."

CHAPTER THREE

Susan's eyes brightened as she listened to my story. "I remember every moment of it," I said. "On that second morning, I woke early and was up as soon as it was light."

I had washed in cold water that I poured from the china jug into the matching basin then I got dressed. My tummy was turning somersaults as I tiptoed into the nursery. I didn't want to wake Princess Vicky, but I was so excited about meeting her for the first time.

The princess was already awake. There, sitting on Mrs Roberts's knee, was a dear little round-faced baby girl with light brown hair. She was wearing the most beautiful dress I had ever seen. It was pure white with lace frills around the neck, at the bottom hem and at the cuffs. Her big blue eyes looked up at me curiously as if to say, "I don't know who you are."

I bobbed a curtsy. "Good morning, Mrs Roberts."

Princess Vicky waved her chubby hands at me.

"Hello, Princess Vicky," I said, leaning forward slightly.

She stretched out towards me and the next thing I knew I was holding a royal princess in my arms.

"There," said Mrs Roberts. "She has taken to you already. I knew she would. I saw your letters of recommendation – you seem to have a way with babies."

I felt my face flush at her praise, but I gave the princess a little hug then handed her back.

I soon got into the routine of work, which I shared with Jane. We washed and ironed Vicky's clothes and bed linen, ran up and down stairs to fetch Vicky's meals from the kitchen and cleaned the nursery. The best part of the day was when we had finished our chores and I was allowed to play with Vicky.

"Weren't you nervous playing with a royal baby?" asked Susan.

"Yes, I was to begin with," I said. "But the most nail-biting moment was my first meeting with the queen."

That afternoon, Mrs Roberts took me with her when she carried Vicky downstairs to see her parents.

"Her Majesty wishes to know who is looking after her child," she said.

Queen Victoria and Prince Albert were eating cake and drinking tea. Mrs Roberts and I curtsied then stood by the door. Vicky sat on her mother's knee and banged on the table with a teaspoon. The queen laughed and Princess Vicky banged harder. When Prince Albert had finished his tea he carried Vicky to the window and they looked out into the palace gardens.

Soon, Vicky began to grizzle. Mrs Roberts took her from the prince and we were just about to leave when I heard a voice.

"So you are the new nursery maid?"

I suddenly realized the queen was talking to me. My stomach all of a quiver, I took a step forward and curtsied again. "Yes, Your Majesty."

"What is your name?"

"I am Charlotte, Your Majesty, but people call me Lottie."

"Good, good. And how are you settling in, Lottie? Mrs Southey tells me you come highly recommended."

"Thank you, Your Majesty. I love little children."

"And do you have any brothers and sisters at home?"

"Yes. I have five, all younger than me."

"Five, eh?" She looked up at Prince Albert and smiled. "That's quite a number."

I shuffled my feet.

"And are they all healthy?" the queen asked.

"Yes, thank you, Your Majesty."

I curtsied again, feeling really thrilled.

Queen Victoria had spoken to me. Me! The girl from Nelson Square!

"Cor," Susan chimed in. "You lucky thing!"

"I know…"

The door banged and Cook bustled into the kitchen carrying a large bag of flour, which she plonked on the table.

"You'll be fine," I said to Susan. "I'll come and see you when I have time, but I'd better go now. Mrs Roberts will be wondering where I am."

Then I hurried back upstairs to the nursery.

CHAPTER FOUR

The first Sunday in November was a beautiful sunny day although there was a cold wind. While Mrs Roberts was walking in the palace gardens with Vicky, I threw open the windows and cleaned and tidied the nursery, changed the linen on Vicky's cot and put the dirty sheets aside to take to the laundry. Then I cleared out the grate, laid and lit the fire and closed the window so it was warm for them when they came in.

I had just come back from the laundry after washing the princess's dresses, petticoats and sheets when I heard her high-pitched babble.

"Dadadadada. Bububububu. Abadaba. Mumumum."

"Yes, Vicky." Mrs Roberts spoke in a quiet

voice. I smiled to myself. It sounded as if she understood whatever the princess was trying to say. She carried Vicky into the nursery. She was quite out of breath after climbing all those stairs.

Princess Vicky was dressed in a white cloak and bonnet. Her cheeks were rosy from the chilly wind outside. She waved her chubby hands and stretched out towards me. I held her in my arms and took off her outer clothes. Under her cloak she was wearing a white calf-length dress with three pale blue stripes round the skirt. The pink ribbon round her waist was tied at the back in a bow. Her round face and brown hair made her look remarkably like the queen.

"You look very pretty this morning, little Vicky," I said as I gave her a hug. "I wonder if Mama and Papa will come up to see you today."

"I'm sure they will if Her Majesty is well enough," said Mrs Roberts. "She is very near her time."

I handed Vicky back to her and hung up the cloak and bonnet. Mrs Roberts sat the princess on a rug on the floor and gave her a rag doll and the little gold rattle with a pink coral handle that had belonged to the queen when she was a baby.

Vicky shook the rattle and laughed at the tinkling of the bells. She put it to her mouth, chewed it, dropped it, rolled over onto her front and began to crawl across the floor.

Just then, I heard footsteps on the stairs and into the room walked Queen Victoria. Mrs Roberts and I curtsied low. The queen waved her hand as a sign for us to stand up straight. She looked very tired. Even though she was wearing her flowing long dress, I couldn't help thinking that her tummy had grown even larger since the day before. She turned to Princess Vicky.

"Hello, my dearest child," she cooed. "Who is a very clever little girl?"

The queen's voice was light and musical and Princess Vicky turned. Waving her hands at her mama, she smiled and blew bubbles and a trickle of saliva ran down her chin. Mrs Roberts hurried forward to wipe it away from her mouth.

"Princess Vicky is getting a new tooth, Your Majesty," she said. "That is why she is making a lot of liquid in her mouth."

"A new tooth?" The queen beamed. "Oh, how wonderful!" She bent over the princess. "I said you were a clever girl," she cooed. "How many do you have now?"

"That will make nine, Your Majesty," said Mrs Roberts.

Jane fetched a chair for Queen Victoria, then we stood in a corner and watched the queen play with her little daughter on her knee.

CHAPTER FIVE

A few minutes later, Prince Albert arrived. He picked up Princess Vicky and hugged her, sat down beside the queen and bounced Vicky on his knee. Then he threw her in the air. I held my breath, afraid that he would drop her, but I need not have worried. He caught her safely every time. She squealed and laughed her gurgling laugh, and after several games he calmed down and quietly hugged her again. She smiled and touched his face. You could tell how much they loved each other.

"Hello, *mein Schatzi*," he said. "Soon you will have a little brother or sister. That will be lovely for us all, *nicht wahr?*"

The prince often said little German phrases. After all, he had come over from Germany to marry Queen Victoria. Sometimes I guessed what the words meant, but other times I didn't understand at all.

The queen looked up at me. "Lottie, isn't it?" she asked.

I bobbed another curtsy, amazed that she would bother to talk to me. "Yes, Your Majesty. Thank you for remembering."

"I like to remember everybody's names, if

I can," she said, "especially those who look after my little girl so wonderfully."

"Thank you, Your Majesty." I bobbed again.

"And your brothers and sisters… are they all well?"

"Yes, thank you, Your Majesty, quite well, so Mother tells me in her letters."

"Good, good."

I saw her hand move onto her tummy. She winced and shifted on her chair.

Then she stood up and headed for the door.

"I need to rest. Goodbye, little darling," she said, stroking Vicky's cheek. "Perhaps we will see you at teatime."

Prince Albert gave Vicky one last hug then passed her to Mrs Roberts and followed Queen Victoria downstairs.

"Do you understand the prince's German words, Mrs Roberts?" I asked.

"Some of them," she said. "I know that *mein Schatzi* means 'my little treasure.'"

"How did the queen know about your brothers and sisters?" asked Jane.

"Her Majesty likes to know all about her staff," said Mrs Roberts. "She is a very kind lady, even though she is so busy being our queen."

"I wish the baby would hurry up and come," said Jane.

"I expect the queen wishes that, too," said Mrs Roberts. "She looks weary."

"I wonder if she will have another girl," said Jane.

I shrugged my shoulders. I was never any good at guessing even though I had had plenty of practice with my mother having had so many babies after me.

"I heard that the queen was disappointed at first that she had a girl," Jane whispered.

"They wanted a boy."

"How do you know that?"

Jane tapped the side of her nose and grinned then looked over her shoulder to make sure Mrs Roberts could not overhear her. "One of her maids told me. Apparently, after Vicky was born the queen said to Prince Albert, 'Never mind, the next one will be a prince'. But the princess is such a delight, they are happy now. "

"I wonder why she said 'never mind'," I said. "The main thing is that the child is healthy, isn't it?"

"Yes, but kings and queens always want a son to be the heir to the throne."

"I suppose so."

I hoped the queen wouldn't be disappointed if she had another girl. I know I wouldn't be, not if she was anything like Princess Vicky.

CHAPTER SIX

That afternoon, I was pleased when Mrs Roberts asked me if I would like to take Vicky to see Queen Victoria and Prince Albert on my own.

"Yes, please," I said. I felt very proud that she trusted me with the royal princess. I held Vicky tightly in my arms as I carefully carried her downstairs.

As soon as we entered the sitting room where Queen Victoria and Prince Albert were having their afternoon tea, the queen's dogs rushed to greet us. I had not been used to dogs before coming to work here, and at first they had made me nervous. But they were friendly animals, and Prince Albert kept a firm watch over them. Before they could come sniffing round me, he called them.

"*Komm*, Eos. *Komm*, little terriers."

The dogs were very obedient. They quickly turned, trotted to him then went to sit down near the queen. She was resting on a sofa with her feet up on a stool. She reached out and petted the dogs in turn. I could tell that she loved them. Mrs Roberts had told me that Her Majesty used to have a King Charles spaniel called Dash. He had been her pet since her childhood, but he died just after Princess Vicky was born. The queen must have been very sad.

Curtsying, I passed Vicky to her Papa then stepped back against a wall. Prince Albert gave Vicky a few tiny pieces of his cake and played with her for about half an hour. The princess laughed and chattered in her babyish way.

"Bravo, dear Albert!" the queen called. "Vicky is having such fun with her papa!"

After that, Vicky sat on her mama's lap for a while until it was time to take her back to the nursery.

I couldn't help wondering what the new baby was going to be like. Girl or boy, would it be as charming as Princess Vicky? She had always been what some people call a good baby, smiley and quiet, only crying when something was really wrong, and great fun to play with.

I could tell that Prince Albert and Queen Victoria were really proud of her and I couldn't help admiring them. They were very busy people, always meeting with the Prime Minister, Sir Robert Peel, or signing papers; going to the Houses of Parliament or welcoming important people to the palace, but they never missed their daily time with Vicky.

Back in the nursery, I played with the princess until her tea was ready. I knew lots of baby games and songs that my little brothers and sisters loved. Vicky loved them, too, and I had taught her some nursery rhymes. I sang one of her favourites.

'Pat-a-cake, pat-a-cake, Baker's Man.
That I will, Master, as fast as I can.
Roll it and prick it and mark it with V
Toss it in the oven for Vicky and me.'

"Bakabakabaka," sang Vicky, copying me and clapping her hands while I sang, and laughing whenever she heard her name. Then we played 'Peek-a-boo'. I loved to hear her squeal with delight each time I popped out from behind my hands.

Soon it was her bath time, the most amusing time of day. While Mrs Roberts undressed Vicky, Jane and I fetched jugs of warm water from downstairs in the kitchens to fill the little oval bath. We tested it with our elbows to make sure it was not too hot for the princess. We needed to spread plenty of towels underneath the bath table because she splashed so much the water slopped everywhere. I was glad of the waterproof apron I wore!

Mrs Roberts gently held Vicky's arm so she didn't slip. When the princess had been washed, she lifted her out of her bath and patted her dry.

"Would you like to sing to her again, Lottie?" Mrs Roberts asked when Vicky was dressed in her nappy and long nightdress.

"Yes, please." I was so glad I had learned nursery rhymes from my own mother. I jigged Vicky on my knee while I sang,

'Ride a cock horse to Banbury Cross
To see what Vicky can buy;
A penny white loaf
A penny white cake
And a two-penny apple pie.'

Vicky laughed and jigged herself up and down.

"Time for a quieter song now," said Mrs Roberts when we had finished. "She needs to relax before she goes to bed."

I nodded and, cradling the little princess, I sang,

'Rock a bye baby
Thy cradle is green
Father's a nobleman
Mother's a queen;
And Betty's a lady
And wears a gold ring
And Johnny's a drummer
And drums for the King.'

I felt Princess Vicky's body relax as her eyes slowly closed. It was a wonderful feeling to know she had fallen asleep in my arms.

Just then, I noticed Prince Albert standing in the doorway. I hadn't heard him coming although I knew he loved to visit Vicky at bath time or bedtime. Seeing him there, I felt embarrassed. He must have been listening to me singing. It made me feel clumsy and I was suddenly terrified of dropping the princess, but he spoke kindly to me.

"You have a very *gut* voice," he said with a smile. "And you will soon have another little one to sing to, *Gott* willing."

"Thank you, Your Royal Highness." I curtsied and felt my face grow hot.

When he had gone and Princess Vicky was fast asleep in her cot, I couldn't help thinking about how different life was for royalty and the upper classes. Even though I admired Queen Victoria and Prince Albert for making sure they saw her every day, it seemed so strange that they only spent such a short time with her and they didn't do all the things poorer parents did for their own children.

What a contrast to Susan's life! She told me once that her whole family lives in one room in an old tumble-down house in Devil's Acre. Buckingham Palace must seem even more amazing to her than it does to me. Her family have a cold tap out in the back yard and share the privy with several other families. They never have enough to eat. She hates to see her little brothers and sisters go hungry and she sends her wages home so they can have better meals.

I think myself lucky that my family is quite well-off. Father is a lawyer and we have our own home and a few servants to help us. Mother had our nurse to help her with each of her babies, but she always spent most of the time with us during the day and made sure she shared in the fun at bath time.

Vicky didn't seem to mind that she didn't see her parents all the time. She was used to her routine of visiting them each afternoon at teatime and she beamed and clapped her hands when they came to the nursery.

That night, when we were getting ready

for bed, I whispered to Jane, "Do you think Princess Vicky will like having a new baby brother or sister?"

"I don't know. Maybe she'll be jealous."

"Maybe," I said.

"Do you think it will be a boy or girl?"

"That's the exciting part of people expecting babies," I said. "Even with a royal baby, there is no way of finding out what it is. You can only make a guess and find out when it arrives."

I blew out the candle and snuggled down under the covers.

"Well, I think it's going to be another girl," Jane whispered.

"I'm not so sure," I whispered. "Goodnight."

CHAPTER SEVEN

I woke with a start. The room was as black as a crow's wing. Gripping my covers, I strained my ears to listen. What had woken me? Then I heard a faint tapping noise.

"Jane," I whispered.

Jane didn't stir.

"Jane!"

"What?" Her voice was full of sleep.

"I heard a noise. It woke me up."

"I expect it's one of the servants up early," said Jane. "Go back to sleep."

But I couldn't. I lay in my bed as rigid as a plank, waiting for another sound. There is was again. Suddenly, I gasped.

"What now?" muttered Jane.

"I've just had a horrible thought," I said, feeling shivers creeping up my neck. "You don't think it could be the boy Jones again, do you?"

"Oh no! I do hope not! It was so terrifying! I'll never forget it."

I pulled my covers tighter around me, remembering what the boy Jones – whose name, we later learned, was Edward – had done. He had broken into Buckingham Palace three times already, but only once since I had come to work here. Nobody knew how he got in, but there are so many windows and doors, maybe he managed to find one unlocked.

On that night of his third break-in, I had been woken by loud voices.

"Quick!" someone shouted. "Catch the villain!"

"Call the guard!"

Shivering in our nightgowns, Jane and I

had slipped out onto the landing in the darkness. We had heard running footsteps. Then more shouts and a loud cry.

"Got him!"

We learned afterwards that the servants had found him in the royal apartments. He had raided the pantry and was sitting as bold as brass tucking in to meat pie and potatoes.

After that, Jane had told me about his two other visits.

"Princess Vicky was only ten days old the second time he got in," she said. "He prowled around the palace, went in the Throne Room and sat on the queen's throne. In the end, he was discovered under a sofa in the queen's sitting room."

I shuddered at the thought of him being so close to the queen. He could have harmed her.

"The queen must have been very frightened," I said.

"I believe she was."

"I would have been."

"Me, too," said Jane. "But his first visit was really strange. He was caught by one of the servants and... you'll never guess what..."

She was teasing me again. I held my breath while I waited for her to finish. Although the thought of boy Jones roaming around at night was horrifying, I was fascinated.

"...he had some of Queen Victoria's underwear stuffed down his trousers!"

I would have laughed if it had not been so terrible.

After the boy Jones's last break-in, we had all felt so relieved when we heard he had been sent away to sea, but I couldn't help wondering if he would come back. In fact, the next time I took Vicky to visit her Mama I peered under the furniture in case he was still there.

Lying in bed in the darkness, I shuddered at the thought of a stranger roaming about in the palace. Surely he couldn't have come back for a fourth visit?

"What should we do?" whispered Jane.

"We had better go and see."

I heard a rustling sound from Jane's bed, then the scrape of a match. I blinked in the brilliant light as she lit a candle. Pulling a shawl around my shoulders, I followed Jane out onto the little landing.

"Let's check on Princess Vicky first," I whispered.

All was quiet in the nursery. Mrs Roberts was there with the princess. They were both fast asleep. So we crept to the top of the stairs and peered down. Someone was hurrying along a corridor down below. My shoulders tensed up as I gripped the banister rail.

"Who's there?" whispered Jane.

A familiar face looked up at us.

"It's only me." In the flickering candlelight I could just make out my friend, Mary.

I felt the tension drain away. "Is it the baby?" I asked.

"No." Mary ran halfway up the stairs. "We did call the doctor because Her Majesty felt very unwell, but it was another false alarm.

He's gone now."

"What's the time?" Jane asked.

"Almost six o'clock."

It was time to get up. Jane and I had our early morning chores to do.

CHAPTER EIGHT

By the time we were ready for work, there was still no news from the queen's chambers.

When Princess Vicky woke up, I took off her nightdress and removed her dirty nappy. She kicked her legs vigorously, enjoying the freedom from the thick wet towelling cloth and oiled waterproof over-knickers that kept the rest of her clothes dry. After I had washed her, she bounced on my knee, blew bubbles and chuckled when I tickled her under her arms.

"I wonder if you will have a new baby brother or sister today," I whispered.

"Bababa," she gurgled.

Vicky's clothes were laid out ready to put on, but it was one of my duties to go down to the kitchens to fetch her breakfast so I passed her to Jane to put on a clean nappy and dress her. I didn't mind Jane taking over because I loved to visit the kitchen with its wonderful smell of freshly baked bread every morning.

Also, going to the kitchen meant I could talk to the other maids of my age for a few seconds. I wondered how Susan was doing.

Susan was busy at the sink, washing dishes. She smiled at me. Her face wasn't quite so thin now and she had some colour in her cheeks. I smiled back, glad she was settling in all right.

Cook was bustling about, all of a fluster.

"I don't know whether I'm coming or going," she said, fanning herself with a cloth. "Not knowing when this new baby will make an appearance. How can I cook when I don't know how many people will require breakfast today?"

I knew she didn't expect an answer and it was best to let her mutter away to herself when she was so agitated. I shrugged my shoulders and fetched a tray from a cupboard. Cook placed two covered dishes and a little china cup on it.

"If only the baby would make up its mind," she said. "Then we'd all know where we were."

As I was leaving the kitchen, Susan sidled up to me. "Did you hear anything in the night, Lottie?" she whispered. "Someone told me the doctor had been called out again."

I nodded, but didn't say anything. Although I loved to hear the gossip, I wasn't one to spread it. I didn't want to say anything that might lose me my job.

When I reached the nursery, Princess Vicky was sitting in the wooden high chair. She looked lovely in a clean pink and white dress. I handed the tray to Mrs Roberts. She lifted one of the lids.

"Ah, scrambled eggs," she said. "Vicky will be pleased. She takes after her Mama. Her Majesty has eggs every day. It doesn't matter how they are cooked... boiled, poached, scrambled, fried, omelette... she loves them all."

She began to feed the princess who opened her mouth wide for each spoonful.

I hurried down to the laundry room and found half a dozen nappies, three vests and two dresses where I had hung them to dry the day before.

There were two flat irons by the fire. Picking one up, I tested it to check it was hot enough to use by spitting on my finger and lightly touching it on the smooth surface of the iron. *Tsss!* My spittle sizzled to tell me the iron was hot.

The nappies and vests only took me a few minutes to iron, but the little dresses took a lot longer. I had to concentrate hard on the frills and tucks. I would be in deep trouble if I scorched them.

My mother had taught me how to iron when I was about eight years old, as she had taught me to sew and knit and all the other skills girls are expected to know.

Princess Vicky had finished her breakfast

when I returned to the nursery. She was sitting on the floor with her ragdoll. I would really have loved to crouch down and play with her, but I still had my chores to do. Back down the stairs I went with her empty breakfast dishes. I was glad I was young and fit or all that running up and down stairs would have exhausted me!

I was climbing back up from the kitchen once again a few minutes later when I heard voices in the nursery. Queen Victoria and Prince Albert were there and they sounded in a very jolly mood. I wondered what was going on.

CHAPTER NINE

I stood outside the nursery door, listening. "Well done, *mein Schatzi!*" I heard Prince Albert say. Then he laughed.

"Clever girl!" the queen giggled. She must have been feeling better after calling out the doctor in the night.

I soon found out what was happening. I pushed open the door and peered inside. The queen was sitting at the side of the room with Prince Albert standing beside her. They were both watching Princess Vicky. She was in the middle of the room seated in the strangest contraption I had ever seen. I stared. It was a kind of woven basket with holes for her legs to go through. The basket had four rods underneath and on the bottom of each rod there was a little wheel.

Vicky was beaming up at her parents. Her feet just reached the floor and she was pushing herself backwards across the room.

Mrs Roberts beckoned me to come in. I curtsied to the queen and prince.

"Do you like our dear little Vicky's new go cart, Lottie?" the queen asked. She shifted in her chair, frowning and running her hand over her belly.

"Yes, very much, Your Majesty," I said. "And it looks as if she likes it, too."

"Prince Albert sent for it," she said, smiling at her husband. "Isn't he the kindest and most generous of papas? It came all the way from Paris in France."

"It really is amazing," I said, curtsying again.

The prince bent down and pushed Vicky gently forward.

"Do you think I am a kind papa?" he asked her.

The little princess pushed backwards again
with her feet and waved her arms, smiling
happily and dribbling down her chin.

"Papa!" she said.

Prince Albert gasped and turned to the
queen. "Did you hear that, my dear? That
was her first real word. She said 'Papa'!"

"Papa! Papa!" said Princess Vicky.

"Oh, my darling little girl!" Prince Albert
knelt down and hugged his daughter then
looked round at the queen. He frowned.

"Are you all right, my dear?" he asked. "You look very uncomfortable."

"I am a little tired," said the queen.

I wasn't sure if I was allowed to feel sorry for a queen, but I couldn't help it. I thought of my mother each time she had expected a baby, how she grew larger and larger and looked more and more tired each day as she waited for her confinement.

I was only two years old when my sister Sarah was born so I have no memory of that, but I will never forget our sadness after the birth of John, who died when he was a few hours old, and after that, the happiness at the safe delivery of Elizabeth, then twins, Annie and William, and lastly Robert, who was still only three. I missed them all.

Since I had come to work for the royal family, I had only been home a few times on my days off. Each time, my brothers and sisters crowded around me and asked a thousand questions. I told them all about the princess and how she was changing from a baby to a little girl. They laughed when I described some of the things she did.

One day, I told my family the news.

"I guess they would like a boy," said Mother. "They want a future King."

"Has it always been like that?" asked Sarah. "About wanting boys, I mean."

"I think so," said Mother. "There have only been a few queens before Victoria, and that was only when there were no boys to take the throne."

"Like Queen Elizabeth," said Elizabeth with a smile.

We all cried when I left and I promised I would go home again as soon as I could. I wondered how many children Queen

Victoria would have and if Princess Vicky would love her brothers and sisters as much as I loved mine.

The queen stood up and took Prince Albert's arm. It was time for them to leave. When they had gone downstairs, I whispered to Jane, "How much longer do you think this royal baby will be?"

"It can't possibly be long now," said Jane.

I couldn't wait.

CHAPTER TEN

It was another fine day, so after Princess Vicky had had a short nap, I dressed her in her cloak and bonnet and Mrs Roberts carried her downstairs. It was my turn to go out with them while Jane cleaned and aired the nursery.

I followed Mrs Roberts to a side door of the palace where the princess's other new contraption waited for her. This was another invention, a three-wheeled kind of chair with a handle. Some people might call it a 'baby-carriage', but I supposed it could also be called a 'push-chair'.

Mrs Roberts sat Princess Vicky inside and covered her legs with a blanket.

"I think we should not stray far from the palace today in case there is any news of the baby," said Mrs Roberts. "We'll stay in the palace gardens."

"Good," I said with a smile. "I love the gardens. They're so peaceful even though we're in the centre of the city."

We walked around the lake in the sunshine and into the shade of a small wood. The trees were wearing their autumn colours and a few leaves drifted down around us. Vicky pointed her little chubby finger and laughed.

Suddenly, as we came out into the sunshine again, we heard a loud screeching cry. It made me jump and the princess's bottom lip began to quiver.

"It's all right," said Mrs Roberts, reaching for her hand. "It's only a peacock."

From behind a bush stalked the most beautiful bird. It had a bright turquoise body, a thin neck and small head with a little fan of feathers on top. I had seen the queen's

peacocks before, but I could never stop myself staring at the brilliant blue patterns in its tail – they looked like hundreds of eyes. The peacock shook its tail, making it ripple like a sparkling river, then it walked past us with its beak in the air.

I bent my knees so I was level with Vicky. "It's a peacock," I said.

Vicky pointed. "Pacapaca." She clapped her hands and chuckled. She was not frightened of the bird, just the noise it had made.

We saw two more peacocks and several silver pheasants as we walked on, then as we turned a corner we came face to face with a very grand lady and her lady-in-waiting. I recognised the grand lady at once. It was Queen Victoria's mother, the Duchess of Kent. We curtsied low. She ignored me, but she nodded to Mrs Roberts then bent over the baby carriage.

"Hello, my pretty little granddaughter," she said.

Princess Vicky looked up at her and smiled.

"How long do we all have to wait before your mama gives you your new brother or sister?" she asked.

It was the question everyone was asking.

We curtsied again and the duchess walked on.

"Time to go back inside," said Mrs Roberts. "We don't want Vicky to catch a chill, do we?"

On the way into the palace, we met Mrs Southey, the Superintendent of the nursery. I had only met her a few times and I was still very nervous of her. I was glad she didn't spend all of her time at Buckingham Palace. She had a thin wrinkly face and piercing grey eyes. She peered over her eyeglasses at me as if I was an insect. I felt my stomach churn. She made me nervous, as if I was back at my interview.

CHAPTER ELEVEN

I had seen the advertisement for a nursery maid in the newspaper. It asked for a girl with experience of caring for babies and young children. Well, I had always helped mother and our nurse to look after my little brothers and sisters.

Besides that, on Saturdays, I had been helping out at Snedden Hall, looking after Lord and Lady Snedden's three little children. I sometimes helped give them their lunch and often played with them in the garden. Their favourite game was hide-and-seek. Freddie, the youngest boy, was a little terror! When I helped their nurse to bathe him, he had such fun splashing me.

On Sundays, I used to help at the Sunday School. I read the Bible to the children and

helped them learn passages of the scriptures –
and if any of the little ones cried, I cuddled
them until their mothers came for them.

I wrote a letter to the head of the nursery
in my very best handwriting. Mother showed
me how to write about who I am and
what I can do without sounding boastful.
Lady Snedden and the vicar wrote letters
to recommend me, too.

I put the three letters into the paper
envelope, sealed it and stuck on a little Penny
Red stamp. I crossed my fingers for luck and
gave it to the Bellman to be posted.

A few days later, I rushed to the door when I saw the postman walking towards the house. He handed me a letter with my name on it in bold handwriting. I felt bubbles tickling inside my tummy as I opened it.

"What does it say?" Mother asked.

"It's an invitation to go for an interview! Oh, Mother, I'm so happy!"

On the day of my interview, I woke even earlier than usual. I put on my Sunday best dress, coat and bonnet, but my hands were shaking so much I could hardly fasten my clothes or the buttons on my boots.

"Keep calm," Mother said. "You'll be fine."

I wished I could believe her.

We sat in a small room with four other girls and their mothers. One by one, the girls were called into the next room and came out looking wide-eyed and white-faced. I was left until last. I was shaking so much by then I was sure I would not be able to curtsy properly.

Suddenly, I heard my name. I shot out of my chair and rushed into a large room where I came face to face with three ladies sitting behind a table. I managed a very wobbly curtsy. The lady in the middle was about as old as my grandmother, but not nearly as friendly.

"I am Mrs Southey," she said, peering at me over her eyeglasses. "I am Superintendent of the nursery."

She asked me lots of questions about myself, my family, housework, sewing and my experience with babies and little children. At first, my tongue seemed dry and too big for my mouth, and I couldn't speak properly, but when one of the other ladies smiled at me I felt better and answered the questions as well as I could.

"You need to know the duties of a nursery maid," said the smiley lady, who, I found out later, was Mrs Roberts. "If you are chosen, you would work up in the nursery, but a lot of your time would be spent cleaning, and washing and ironing the princess's clothes. How do you feel about that?"

I swallowed. "I can do all of those things," I said. "I've helped our maid at home, but I was hoping I could help look after the little princess, too."

"Of course you would help look after her," said Mrs Southey, briskly. "She is only a few months old. She needs a lot of care."

"You have two good letters to recommend you, Charlotte," said the smiley lady. "You seem to be a good worker, are very good with children and have a pleasant character. Thank you for coming."

"We will write to you," said Mrs Southey.

"Thank you," I said, then I bobbed another curtsy and dashed from the room.

I had to wait for more than a week before I heard from the palace, but at last another letter arrived. My little brothers and sisters clung round my skirts, jumping up and down with excitement when they saw it.

"Open it!"

"What does it say?"

I dared not open it. I would be so disappointed if they had not chosen me.

Mother gently took the letter from my trembling hands. She unfolded it and handed it back to me. I read it. Then read it again and a third time, just to make sure. I sat down heavily in a chair and burst into tears.

"Oh dear, Lottie," said Mother, putting her arms round my shoulders. "I'm so sorry. You did your best."

I shook my head. Then I started laughing through my tears.

"It says 'We have selected you to be the new Royal Nursery Maid.' Oh Mother, I'm so happy. I'll be paid £10 per year. And they want me to start on Monday at Buckingham Palace!"

Suddenly, Mrs Southey's voice brought me back to the present.

"I trust this young girl is still performing her duties in a satisfactory manner?" she asked Mrs Roberts.

"Oh yes, Mrs Southey." Mrs Roberts beamed at me. "Better than that. Lottie is an excellent nursemaid."

I had such a warm feeling as we went inside and thought there was nobody in the whole world as lucky as me.

CHAPTER TWELVE

That afternoon, Queen Victoria and Prince Albert came to see Vicky again. I kept looking at the queen. She was much quieter than usual and she looked very pale.

Much later, when we were snuggled in our beds, I whispered to Jane, "I think Her Majesty is going to have her baby tonight."

"What makes you think that?"

"She was very quiet this afternoon... and she didn't play with Vicky."

"Well? That doesn't mean anything."

"I know, but she kept frowning and once I thought I saw her wince in pain."

"She's had so many false alarms," said Jane. "This could be another one."

I didn't answer. I just had this feeling that I was right.

It happened again. Jane and I were woken by noises from downstairs. But this time I somehow knew that it was not Edward Jones and it was not another false alarm.

"The queen's in labour," I whispered.

"How do you know that?"

"I don't know how… but I'm sure she is."

Jane lit the candle and we shivered as we slipped from our beds, wrapped our shawls around us and opened the door. Tiptoeing to the top of the stairs, we peered downwards. The lower landing was lit by a line of oil lamps.

A maid hurried by, but she looked much too busy to stop and talk to us.

"I think you may be right," Jane whispered. I realized my legs were shaking.

"I feel a bit dizzy," I whispered.

Jane giggled. "It's not you having the baby!" she said.

I smiled. "I know, silly! But I used to feel like this when my mother had her babies... I suppose I can't help being worried as well as excited."

At that moment, another maid walked quickly towards us. It was Mary. I leant over the banisters.

"Psst!"

She looked up, startled and then grinned.

"Can't stop...I've got to fetch Mrs Lilly."

"Mrs Lilly! The midwife!" said Jane.

"I knew it!" I said. "The baby is coming at last!"

I heard the clock strike five, but Jane and I were both too excited to go back to sleep. We went to our bedroom and got washed and dressed. It was too early to wake Vicky or Mrs Roberts, but I felt so giddy and jittery I had to do something to occupy myself. We went down to the laundry room. The fire had been lit under the giant copper, which was filled to the brim with water. I knew that hot water was always called for when babies were being born.

I washed some of Vicky's nappies while Jane ironed a dress. Then we went back up to the nursery to see if Mrs Roberts was awake. She was.

"Where have you two been?" she asked with a frown.

I opened my mouth to apologize, but she didn't give me a chance.

"I presume you have heard… Mrs Lilly is

here. She has sent for Doctor Lucock. The queen is in labour. We have much to do."

While Jane washed and dressed Princess Vicky, Mrs Roberts gave me a list of jobs. First, I had to make sure the royal cradle was perfectly dusted and polished. It had not been used since Vicky was a small baby and it was stored in a cupboard at the end of the landing. When I opened the cupboard door I gasped. The cradle was amazing.

It was shaped like a deep wooden boat, painted deep gold. It hung inside a wooden frame with a strong base, two straight poles at the cradle's ends and an arched pole over the top. I touched the cradle and it swung gently inside its frame. Hooked onto the arched pole was a deep gold curtain, which could be pulled across and around the baby. It would be needed now it was November and the nights were getting colder.

I had to tug hard to get the cradle out of the cupboard and along to the nursery. Jane had been downstairs to fetch Vicky's breakfast.

"That's a cradle fit for a prince or princess!" she said. "I remember when Vicky slept in it. I used to rock her to sleep."

I smiled, but I wished I could have seen Princess Vicky tucked up inside. "Any news?" I asked.

"No, just that Doctor Lucock is here. He's staying this time."

It was still only about eight o'clock so I guessed the baby would not be born yet, but I was worried. The doctor had been so many times in the past few weeks, even when we were at Windsor. Was the baby going to be all right?

CHAPTER THIRTEEN

While I cleaned the cradle for the new baby, I thought about Windsor Castle. We often travel there because Queen Victoria loves it so much. Our latest visit had begun early in September, when the first spots of orange and gold had begun to show on the trees. We stayed at Windsor for several weeks.

I could understand why the queen loved being at the castle. It was a massive place with grey stone walls and high towers surrounded by lovely countryside. From my tiny bedroom in a turret I could see such beautiful gardens with flower beds, statues, lawns and a huge round pond in the middle. Beyond that there was the Great Park and a forest.

I remembered Her Majesty riding through the Great Park in her carriage pulled by four dashing white horses. In the evenings, I heard music and laughter. Many actors and musicians came to perform to Queen Victoria and Prince Albert.

The queen and the prince worked hard at Windsor, as they did every day in London. The Prime Minister and other members of the government had to travel out for meetings with them. Queen Victoria still had to rule the country, with Prince Albert's help, even if they loved to have fun, too.

But Her Majesty had felt unwell several times while we were there. Luckily, Doctor Lucock was staying in the castle, too, so he came immediately each time she sent for him. Then one day, when we had been at Windsor for five weeks, the queen felt quite ill. My friend Mary was in the room when the doctor came in, and she told me what he said.

"You must return to London immediately, Your Majesty. The baby could come early. There is always a danger of losing premature babies."

That worried me. I remembered poor little John, my dead brother, and thought how terrible it would be if that happened to our queen.

We had all rushed back to Buckingham Palace the next day, but three weeks had passed since then. I prayed that the baby would be healthy and not too small.

I stood back when I had finished cleaning the cradle, pleased with my work. It was spotless and the curtains hung without creases.

"Good work, Lottie," said Mrs Roberts. "Now all we need is a baby to go inside it."

She had allowed Jane to go downstairs for more news.

"I've just seen the Duchess of Kent," Jane said when she came back. "She is pacing up and down like a caged lion."

I had never seen a lion, but I could imagine how worried the duchess was about her daughter.

"Baroness Lehzen is there, too, looking

nervous. All the servants are so busy, fetching hot water, giving drinks to the important people who keep arriving…"

"Important people?" I thought it was a strange time for guests to come to the palace.

"Yes. The Prime Minister has just arrived with several other Members of Parliament. The Bishop of London is here, too, but they are still waiting for the Archbishop of Canterbury. He's expected soon."

"Why are they all coming here now?" I asked.

"Because as soon as a royal baby is born, it has to be shown to members of the government and the church to prove that it is the queen's child," said Mrs Roberts. "They have to make sure that nobody swaps the baby over, especially as they want a boy to be the next king."

"That's silly," I said. "Nobody is going to

swap babies, are they?"

"Not today, perhaps. But in the olden days, this sometimes happened. In fact, the important people of the land had to be inside the room to witness the birth."

I pulled a face. "That would be dreadful. My mother had nobody except the midwives to help her."

"But your mother isn't queen," said Jane with a grin. She always managed to make me smile.

Vicky had finished her breakfast, but she was still sitting in her high chair. She banged on the top of it with her spoon as if to tell us off. We were not paying any attention to her. I bobbed a little curtsy and smiled at her.

"Sorry, Vicky," I said. "We were talking about your mama."

"Mamamamamama," gurgled Vicky and she banged the spoon down again.

I was ready to play with her, but Mrs Roberts called me.

"Lottie, you haven't finished those tasks I set you. Time is marching on. We don't want the baby to be born before we are ready."

"Yes, Mrs Roberts," I said and hurried to find the tiny clothes the baby would wear. We had washed and ironed them all, but they were tucked away in a drawer. At first, my hands were shaking and I felt fidgety, but sorting the clothes helped to calm me. I couldn't believe how many layers babies had to wear.

I pulled open the drawer and took out the clothes one by one. First there was the bellyband. It was about a yard long and made of woollen flannel. It had to be wrapped round and round the baby's body to keep it warm. Then I found the towelling nappies and pilches. These were semi-waterproof triangles made of thick flannel. They were worn on top of a nappy to protect the baby's other clothes.

Next I lifted out a shirt made of the finest cotton that would feel soft on the delicate skin of the baby's shoulders. The strangest thing was the woollen barracoat, with a short, sleeveless top part and a very long pleated skirt that should be about six inches longer than the baby. The cotton petticoat and nightgown were also long enough to cover the baby's feet. Lastly, I found a tiny white cap for the baby's head.

I laid these clothes in a basket ready to be taken downstairs with the cradle when the nurses asked for them.

After that, Jane and I took it in turns to nip downstairs for the latest news in between our everyday chores and playing with Vicky.

"Prince Albert hasn't been up to see Vicky today," I said to Jane when she came back upstairs after her turn. "I wonder where he is."

She coughed and looked at the floor.

"What's the matter?" I asked.

"Mary told me he's in the queen's chamber with the queen," she said

I gasped. "Men never go near their wives when they're in childbirth…. except the doctor, of course."

"Mary said the queen wanted the prince to be with her," said Jane. "Well, she *is* queen so she can have whatever she wants, can't she?"

"I suppose so," I said, but I turned my hot face away from Jane. I didn't want her to notice my blush.

It was my turn to go down. As I reached the bottom of the stairs I looked at the clock. It said twelve minutes to eleven o'clock.

Suddenly, I heard a sound. I froze, listening, wondering if I had imagined it. There it was again, a high-pitched squall. The baby!

CHAPTER FOURTEEN

Everyone dashed about, bumping into each other, shaking hands, patting each other on the back.

"Thank God for a safe delivery!"

"Is it a boy or a girl?"

"We'll soon find out."

I leapt two steps at a time up to the nursery.

"The baby!" I panted. "It's been born. I just heard it squall."

"Thank heavens!" said Mrs Roberts.

"Boy or girl?" asked Jane.

"I don't know. I'll go and find out."

I dashed back downstairs, not giving Jane the chance to say it was her turn.

Nobody noticed me as I crept like a shadow into the room where the prime minister and the other important people were standing. I saw the Duchess of Kent and Baroness Lehzen. They both looked happy, but they were both staring at the door to the queen's chamber. I knew I could be in trouble if I was caught. A lowly nursemaid like me should not be there, but I could not stop myself. I had heard the baby cry – now I wanted to see it.

Silently, I slid behind a long curtain and waited. A few minutes later, I heard a door open. Everyone stopped talking. The room was silent. I peered through a gap in the curtain. A nurse walked into the room holding a white bundle in her arms. Prince Albert was right behind her.

The Prime Minister stepped forward.

"We are glad for the safe delivery of this child," he said. "Is it a boy or a girl?"

The nurse unwrapped the baby for a moment and showed the naked body.

"A boy, *Gott sei Dank*," said Prince Albert, smiling. "The queen and I are delighted."

As if to prove he was ready to be the future king, the baby opened his mouth wide and let out such a loud squall for such a tiny person. Everybody chuckled.

"God bless the new prince!" said the Bishop of London.

The nurse wrapped the white sheet around the baby, then turned and left the room. Prince Albert nodded to the Duchess of Kent who followed him and the nurse and closed the door behind her.

At that moment, the Archbishop of Canterbury rushed in, red-faced and panting.

"So sorry..." he muttered. "Am I too late?"

I sneaked out of the room and leapt upstairs three steps at a time.

"It's a boy!" I yelled as I ran into the nursery. "I've seen him. He's a big baby and he has a loud cry."

"We heard him from up here," said Mrs Roberts. "This is wonderful news."

She stepped forward and hugged me. I hugged her back although I was so surprised.

She had never touched me before except for shaking my hand when I first met her. But a new prince isn't born every day! Mrs Roberts hugged Jane then she held Princess Vicky in her arms and hugged her, too.

"You have a new baby brother," said Mrs Roberts.

Vicky looked at her and smiled although I knew she didn't understand what Mrs Roberts had told her. How could she? The dear little thing was not quite one year old.

"I wonder what they will call him," said Jane.

"Albert," I said, "after his father."

"George," said Jane. "After the queen's grandfather."

"William," I said. "Or Charles."

"Or maybe Edward," said Jane. "Queen Victoria's father, the Duke of Kent, was Edward, wasn't he, Mrs Roberts?"

"Yes, I believe so. Well, we will have to wait and see."

At that moment, Prince Albert bounded into the room. We all curtsied. The prince had such a happy smile on his face. He reached for Vicky then held her high above his head and looked up at her.

"Have you heard, *mein Schatzi*?" he asked. "Did you know you have a handsome baby brother?"

"Babababa," said Princess Vicky and she gurgled with laughter.

"How is Her Majesty, Your Royal Highness?" asked Mrs Roberts.

"She is very well, *Gott sei Dank*, but she needs me by her side. The Duchess of Kent is with her at the moment and I expect Baroness Lehzen will want to see her and our baby prince."

He hugged Princess Vicky to his chest

and waltzed around the room. Then he gave her a big kiss on her cheek.

"I will not stay any longer," he said and handed Vicky to me. I curtsied as I took her.

"Take *gut* care of my pretty princess," he said.

"Yes, Your Royal Highness."

"Shall we bring her down to see her mama and brother?" asked Mrs Roberts.

"Tomorrow," said the prince. "Yes, tomorrow will be best. The queen needs to rest today."

When he had gone, I looked at Mrs Roberts and Jane. I could tell from their expressions that they were disappointed that we wouldn't be going to see the baby today. At least *I* had already seen him!

A few moments later, Mary came up to the nursery.

"Are the clothes ready for the new prince?"

she asked. "The nurse is asking for them."

Fetching the basket, I handed it to Mary. The clothes looked so tiny and perfectly folded I felt pleased that I had been the one to prepare them.

"Thank you... and we need the cradle, too," said Mary.

"You're so lucky," said Jane. "We're supposed to be the nursemaids, but you are the one who gets the chance to see him."

Mary smiled. "And hear him! He likes the sound of his own voice!"

"We'll see him tomorrow, Jane," said Mrs Roberts. "And we'll get the chance to look after him soon enough."

I watched two servants carry the heavy cradle downstairs. They left it outside the queen's chambers then it was wheeled inside and the door closed.

CHAPTER FIFTEEN

Boom!

The room seemed to shake with the sound. Holding tightly to Vicky, I crouched down on the floor, protecting her with my body. Was Buckingham Palace under attack?

Boom!

Vicky's bottom lip quivered then she burst into tears. Her little body was shaking almost as much as mine.

"Shush! Shush!" I said. "Don't be frightened. I'll look after you."

Boom!

Flinching at each sound, I looked across the room. Jane had ducked under the table, but Mrs Roberts was sitting on a chair looking calm.

"It's all right," she said. "It's only the

cannon announcing the birth of the prince."

"Ah!" I should have realized what it was. I remembered hearing the guns booming in the distance once before. Father had explained it was to announce the birth of Princess Vicky.

Boom!

Slowly, I got up from the floor. Vicky was still crying so I sat down and gently jigged her up and down on my knee. I sang *Baa Baa Black Sheep* then *Jack and Jill Went Up the Hill* while Jane shook the bell rattle.

Boom!

Soon Vicky began to listen to me. She clapped her hands and began to giggle.

Boom!

"How many cannon shots will there be?" Jane asked.

"Forty-one, I expect," said Mrs Roberts.

"Forty-one?"

"Yes, twenty-one to announce the birth of the new prince and an extra twenty because Hyde Park is a Royal Park. And if you listen carefully, you might hear another lot from the Tower of London. I hope so."

Boom!

I knew why Mrs Roberts had said, 'I hope so'. There had been a terrible fire at The Tower of London only ten days ago. I was fast asleep in bed so I didn't know about it until the next morning. Joseph, one of the servants, had been up to Tower Hill to watch.

"The flames were so fierce," he told Jane and me. "The glow could be seen for miles."

"Is it still burning now?" asked Jane.

"No. Firemen and soldiers managed to put it out by three o'clock this morning."

"What about the crown jewels?" I asked.

"A policeman managed to get them all out. He wasn't hurt, but his uniform was charred."

That Sunday had been my day off, so Father and I decided to take a walk past the Tower of London. I was shocked and frightened by what I saw. Several towers were badly damaged and there was ash and smoke everywhere. I couldn't understand how a strong, stone building like that could burn so fiercely.

Boom! Boom! Boom!

At last, the park guns stopped firing and the room became very quiet.

It was much later than usual when I went down to the kitchen for Vicky's lunch. Susan was singing to herself as she scrubbed the wooden draining board. Cook was red-faced and red-eyed. I was just about to ask whatever was wrong when she danced around the table and gave me a kiss on my cheek. Then she burst into tears.

"Oh, I'm so proud to be the Buckingham Palace Cook on such a day as this!" she cried. "I'm so happy for Her Majesty. I remember when I had my tenth baby…"

She stopped and grinned through her tears.

"Sorry, you don't want to hear about that. You've come for the little lady's lunch, haven't you?"

"Yes, please." I smiled at her as she wiped her eyes then she fetched a tray and placed several dishes on it.

"There's a piece of chicken with some nice carrots, cabbage and gravy," said Cook. "I know she likes that."

I smiled and nodded. The little princess had a good appetite.

"Then there's poached pears for her dessert."

"Thank you," I said. "Have you heard how the queen is?"

"Well, Mary came into the kitchen a few minutes ago and she said Her Majesty is very well," said Cook. "She's sleeping… needs to rest. They say the new prince is a bonny lad with a good pair of lungs."

I nodded. "I think the whole palace has heard him."

"No one has seen him yet though."

"I have. I saw him." I clasped my hand over my mouth. I hadn't meant to boast, but I was so excited it just burst out before I could stop it.

"You didn't!" gasped Susan. "How did you manage that?"

I quickly told them about my little adventure behind the curtain then took the tray and carried it up to the nursery.

Vicky had forgotten all about the cannon. She was in her highchair waiting for me, holding her spoon and waving it above her head. She beamed at me as I sat down beside her and she opened her mouth wide for each spoonful, as usual. Every so often she poked her spoon into the dish and splashed some of her lunch onto the floor. Then she leant over and looked at it, laughed and splashed her food again. She was becoming quite a little mischief, but I loved her for it.

When she had finished, it was time for her afternoon nap.

"I'll stay with the princess and tidy up while she is asleep," said Mrs Roberts. "Why don't you two go down to the front of the palace? If the news of a prince has got out, there might be a crowd outside the railings."

"Thank you, Mrs Roberts," we said with a curtsy.

We didn't need telling twice. We dashed down the back stairs, along the corridor and out of a door at the side of the palace. I grabbed Jane's arm.

"Listen," I said.

We stood still. In the distance, I could

hear the *boom, boom, boom* of cannon.

"Mrs Roberts was right," said Jane. "More guns. They must be from the Tower of London."

At that moment, a faint sound of church bells began to ring out across the park. First one church, then another, then another until the air was filled with such a marvellous jumble of music it sent shivers up my spine. Then, mixed with the distant booms and bells, I heard another sound coming from the front of the palace. It was people cheering.

"Come on," I said. "Let's go and see what happening."

We hurried round to the front. A great crowd had gathered outside the railings and stretched as far as I could see.

"There are thousands of people," I gasped. "The news must have spread fast."

Then I spotted an easel standing just inside

the railings. A notice had been placed on the easel, facing the crowd. I peered at the notice. It was one simple sentence announcing the birth of the queen's son. It was signed by Doctor Lucock and several other people.

We peered out through the railings. People were dancing and waving Union Flags. Some were cheering and shouting.

A lady close to me called, "Welcome to our new prince!"

A man shouted, "God save the Queen!"

"God save the Queen!" yelled the crowd.

The excitement of the crowd was catching. It made me shiver. I had to swallow hard or I might have been like Cook and burst into tears. I looked at Jane. She was biting her lip, fighting back tears, too. It was such a magical moment. I'll never forget it as long as I live.

CHAPTER SIXTEEN

"You were right, Mrs Roberts," I panted as I raced ahead of Jane up the back stairs and into the nursery. "You should have seen the crowds."

"Everyone is so excited," said Jane.

"It gave me goose bumps," I said.

Mrs Roberts smiled. "I remember the happy crowds outside the palace when Princess Vicky was born. This time there will be even more celebration as it's a boy."

"Girls are best," Jane said with a grin.

At that moment, Vicky awoke and sat up in her cot. She stretched and yawned and rubbed her eyes then beamed at us all. She waved to Jane and raised her hands to me. I lifted her out and changed her nappy.

"You're a lucky girl," I whispered. "You've

got a dear little baby brother. Think of all the fun you will have playing with him."

"Papa," she said.

"Yes, I expect Papa will come and see you soon," I said. I hoped he would not be too busy to come.

It was Jane's turn to play with Vicky so I took the dirty nappy and some other clothes to the laundry. I scooped hot water and soap into a bowl and washed the clothes, rinsed them in cold water, pushed them through the mangle and hung them up to dry. Then I returned to the nursery and sat in a corner, sewing a new dress for Vicky. My mother had taught me to sew with such small stitches they were almost invisible.

That evening, we went down to the servants' dining room. Everybody was chattering, patting each other on the back, singing, laughing and making merry. All the servants and maids were allowed a glass of wine mixed with whisky, a favourite drink of Her Majesty's, but I refused. I knew my mother and father would not allow me to taste anything so strong. I had apple juice instead.

"A toast!" called the Head Steward. "To Her Majesty, Queen Victoria, and her new baby prince!" We all raised our glasses.

"To Her Majesty, Queen Victoria, and her new baby prince!"

"Joseph has been out to buy a copy of the *London Gazette*," said the Head Steward. "It's a special edition. Show them, Joseph."

Joseph held up the newspaper. In large letters, it said *The London Gazette Extraordinary* and its date was Tuesday November 9th 1841.

"Lottie, read it out to all of us, will you?" The Head Steward was smiling down at me.

I nodded, feeling my face turn crimson as everyone turned to look at me. Then, hands shaking, I picked up the newspaper and began to read.

"Buckingham Palace, November 9th, 1841. This morning, at twelve minutes before eleven, the queen was happily delivered of a prince. His Royal Highness Prince Albert, Her Royal Highness the Duchess of Kent, several Lords of Her Majesty's Most Honourable Privy Council and the Ladies of Her Majesty's Bedchamber, being present."

I paused for breath. There was silence in the room as everyone waited for me to carry on.

"This great and important news was immediately made known to the town by the firing of the Park and Tower guns, and the Privy Council being assembled as soon as possible…" I missed out a few words that were rather long and difficult for me. "… it was ordered that a form of thanksgiving for the queen's safe delivery of a prince be prepared by His Grace, the Archbishop of Canterbury to be used in all churches and chapels throughout England and Wales on Sunday 14th of November…"

"That's next Sunday," whispered the Head Steward, but there was one more sentence to read.

"Her Majesty and the infant prince are, God be praised, both doing well."

"Well done, Lottie," whispered Susan. "I wish I could read like you."

I grinned and bobbed a little curtsy, my face still a deep shade of red.

I didn't stay there long after that. I still had my sewing to finish. Vicky was going to wear the new dress in the morning. It was made of red velvet with lace around the collar and cuffs. I wanted her to look extra pretty when she met her new brother.

CHAPTER SEVENTEEN

My eyes were really tired when I woke next morning. I had worked by candlelight until late, but the dress was finished. My tummy turned a somersault. We were going to meet the new baby prince today.

"Jane!" I said. "Time to get up."

When I was washed and dressed, I went to the laundry room and ironed the washing I had left to dry and brought it back upstairs.

As I passed the queen's chambers I heard the new prince. He was squalling very loudly. Perhaps he was ready for his next feed. He needed lots of milk to help him grow big and strong, especially as one day he would be king.

Princess Vicky was awake when I got back. Dressed in just her underclothes and nappy, she crawled across the floor towards me and pulled herself up on my skirt so she was standing beside me.

"A special day today," I said.

She sat down on her bottom with a bump and beamed up at me.

"You'll be able to meet your new brother."

"Bada," she said.

"I expect Papa will send for us when they are all ready."

"Papa," she said.

When she had eaten her scrambled egg and thrown most of her toast on the floor beneath the high chair, Mrs Roberts dressed her in the red velvet dress. It fitted her perfectly.

"Well done, Lottie," said Mrs Roberts. "You are a fine needlewoman indeed."

I bobbed a curtsy. "Thank you," I said, feeling my face warm up.

At that moment, the door opened and Prince Albert came in.

"Papa!" said Princess Vicky.

"Hello, *mein Schatzi.*" He took her from Mrs Roberts and held her at arms-length. "You do look pretty today. Shall we go now to meet your brother?"

"How is the baby this morning?" Mrs Roberts asked.

"Very well," said Prince Albert. "But he has such a loud voice. The nurse was up most of the night with him."

"And the queen?"

"Her Majesty had a good night, *danke.* She is looking forward to seeing Vicky."

Mrs Roberts, Jane and I followed Prince Albert and Princess Vicky downstairs to the queen's chambers. The curtains were closed in the bedroom, but four oil lamps were burning at the sides of the room. Queen

Victoria was sitting up in the four-poster bed. Prince Albert sat Vicky beside her mama. My fingers tingled and my legs felt wobbly as the nurse walked into the room carrying the baby. He was closely wrapped in a white blanket so I could only see his face. His eyes were closed and he looked peaceful.

"Baba," said Princess Vicky and she pointed at her baby brother.

The nurse curtsied and brought the baby to the queen's bed. As she placed him in the queen's arms, he opened his dark blue eyes. Queen Victoria smiled down at her baby.

"I hope and pray you will grow up to be as good and handsome as your dear papa," she said.

A second later, he opened his mouth wide and squalled loudly. Princess Vicky's bottom lip quivered then she opened her mouth, too, and screamed.

Prince Albert picked up Vicky and hugged her.

"Oh, *mein Schatzi*," he whispered. He looked at the queen. "My dear, I believe our little Vicky is afraid of the baby."

Vicky slowly calmed down, although her little chest was heaving and she stared at the baby as if he were a fierce monster.

My heart beat faster as I watched Vicky clinging to her papa. I was sure he was right. She was scared by her own baby brother. I hoped she would soon grow to love him.

Gently, the nurse took the baby and hurried to the other side of the room. She rocked him in her arms and at last, she managed to calm him and he stopped squalling. I wished that could have been me. I was dying to hold him and I knew I could quieten him with my singing, but I would have to wait. Right now, it was the little princess who needed me most.

We went every day to to visit the baby, and Vicky soon became braver around him. He often cried while we were there, but she learned to ignore the noise.

"Baba," she would say, touching his face and holding his tiny hand. She seemed fascinated by his fingers, poking each one in turn.

A few days after he was born, the nurse brought the baby prince upstairs and I finally got to hold him. I wrapped my arms tightly around him and looked down at his face.

"One day," I whispered as we stood by the window looking out over the palace grounds, "you will be king."

EPILOGUE

Jane and Lottie were right between them about the names the baby prince would have. He was named Prince Albert Edward and everyone called him Prince Bertie.

He was a rather unruly boy and unfortunately Queen Victoria didn't like him very much. He didn't live up to what his father, Prince Albert, expected of him, as the boy who would become king.

When Prince Bertie grew up he married Princess Alexandra of Denmark and they had six children. After Queen Victoria died on 22nd January 1901, Prince Bertie became King Edward VII. By then he was almost 60 years old and reigned for less than 10 years. He died on 6th May 1910.

He was our Queen Elizabeth's great grandfather.